SESAME STREET
Stays Up Late

Based on the television special by Lou Berger
Illustrated by Joe Mathieu
Featuring Jim Henson's Sesame Street Muppets

A Random House PICTUREBACK®

Random House / Children's Television Workshop

Photo credit: Photograph of Tiffy on page 18 © NDR 1995.

On Sesame Street, Gina is played by Alison Bartlett, Savion is played by Savion Glover, and Tarah is played by Tarah Lynne Schaeffer.

Library of Congress Cataloging-in-Publication Data: Berger, Lou. Sesame Street stays up late / based on the television special by Lou Berger ; illustrated by Joe Mathieu. p. cm. — (A Random House pictureback) SUMMARY: The Sesame Street Muppets watch a holiday television program showing how children around the world celebrate the New Year. ISBN 0-679-86743-0 (trade)
[1. New Year—Fiction. 2. Puppets—Fiction.] I. Mathieu, Joseph, ill. II. Title. PZ7.B45213Se 1995 [E]—dc20 94-32232

Manufactured in the United States of America   10 9 8 7 6 5 4 3 2 1

It was December 31st—New Year's Eve!

"It's a very special night," said Big Bird. "We're having a party right here on Sesame Street, and *you're* invited!

"Snuffy's taking a nap so he can stay up late, but he's missing all the fun. Come on, Snuffy, wake up!"

But Snuffy kept on snoozing.

"I can't wait until the clock strikes twelve! That's when this year ends," said Big Bird. "We'll blow horns and shout, 'Happy New Year!'"

"*What?*" cried Telly. "This year is going to *end?* I didn't know that!"

"Don't worry, Telly," said Gina. "New Year's Eve is fun. It's celebrated all over the world! Look." Savion turned on the TV.

"This is the Monster News Network in the U.S.A.," anchor-monster Elmo announced. "Tonight we'll show kids in other countries welcoming the new year. Here is our first report—from Mexico! Are you there, Rosita?"

"¡Hola!" said Rosita from Mexico. "Meet Elmo's cousin Pepe. We're making a piñata with this pot! We'll stuff it with treats and decorate it for tonight's party. It's a tradition!"

"We have special New Year's traditions here, too," Gina told everyone. "In Times Square, a big glittery ball falls from a tall building as the clock strikes twelve."

"Hey, that gives me an idea!" said Big Bird. "We can have a ball fall right here on Sesame Street! Wolfgang can toss a beach ball up in the air."

"And I, the Count, will count down the seconds until the new year begins—starting *now*. 14,747 seconds...14,746 seconds...14,745 seconds... *Wonderful!*" cried the Count.

"Ah-ha-ha!"

Then Elmo-noske, Elmo's cousin in Japan, appeared on television with some friends. They had a big mallet and a bowl.

"We're pounding rice to make New Year's cakes," explained Elmo-noske. He pounded and pounded.

Elmo-noske tasted the rice cakes when they were done. "*Mm-mm,
scrumptious!*" he said. "This is Elmo-noske from Japan wishing you a
sweet and gooey New Year! *Hai!*"

"It's time for anchor-monster Elmo in the U.S.A. to take you to Portugal. Hello, special reporter Tita!"

"Hi there, Elmo!" said Tita from Portugal. "On New Year's Eve here, every child eats twelve grapes and makes twelve wishes—one for each month of the year!

"So long, and may all your New Year's wishes come true!"

Meanwhile, back on Sesame Street, Telly Monster was still worried about the year coming to an end. Then he had a great idea. He dressed up as a Very Important Grownup and made an announcement.

"STOP THAT MERRYMAKING!" Telly boomed. "There can be no New Year's Eve party here! Sesame Street is in a No-Party Zone!"

"No party?" cried Big Bird. "That would be terrible!"
Just then the Very Important Grownup lost his beard, and everyone saw that it was Telly Monster.

"Telly, what are you doing?" asked Gina.

"I thought that if there were no New Year's Eve party, there would be no new year!" cried Telly, running away.

"Telly, wait!" Gina called after him.

"Maybe we can hide from the new year," Telly told his doll, Freddy.

"Shalom, Oofnik and Kippi!" said anchor-monster Elmo to the reporters in the studio in Israel.

"Yeah, okay, this is Oofnik the Grouch. We celebrated the Jewish New Year here three months ago, and here's our report.

"We ate sweet and delicious food in the marketplace. *Yucch.*"

"We listened to the shofar!" added Kippi. "See? That's the ram's horn we blow at the start of each new year."

"My family has its own holiday tradition," Oscar announced from his can back on Sesame Street. "Every year on December 31st, we all talk together on the phone—a grouch conference call!"

Oscar dialed the telephone. "Hi there, Mom!"

"Have a crummy New Year, Son!" she grumbled.

Then Oscar and his mom were connected to Uncle Hank, Aunt Ethel, and Uncle Fred.

"Nyah-nyah-nyaaaah-nyah-nyaah-nyaaah!" whined the grouches together. They all slammed down their phones at the same time.

Oscar cackled. "I love it when the family gets together!"

Then the Monster News Network switched to Germany.

"This is Tiffy Monster," said the reporter. "We're all dressed up in costumes, and we're going from house to house for treats. We bang on pots and sing and shout.

"Good luck in the coming year! Bye-bye!"

Next the show went to the famous ski slopes of Norway.

"Hi! I'm news-monster Alfa," said the reporter. "This is a special New Year's Eve race! The kids race down the hill on skis or sleds. Everyone must zoom across the finish line before the sun goes down...and the sun is sinking fast! Hurry, hurry! Happy New Year!"

Meanwhile, on Sesame Street, Telly was hiding from the new year dressed like a lamp. Gina found him in FINDER'S KEEPERS and gave him a hug.

"You don't have to be afraid, Telly," she said. "New Year's Eve is fun, and I'll be with you."

"Would you hold my hand, Gina, until the ball falls off the seal's nose?" he asked.

"Yes, Telly," she answered.

"Then…let's go to the party!"

The party on Sesame Street was about to begin.

"10...9...8...7 seconds to the new year!" called the Count.

Snuffy was still snoring. Big Bird shook him gently. "Snuffy, wake up! Please! The ball is going to fall!"

"6...5...4," cried the Count, leading the countdown. "3...2...1! Ah-ha-ha!"

And just as Snuffy's big eyes opened, Wolfgang the Seal threw back his head and tossed the ball high into the air.

When the ball finally bounced back down on Sesame Street, everyone shouted with joy.

"Happy New Year!"

Grover staggered in. "I hope I am not too late! I brought you grapes all the way from Portugal...and that was one long swim! Go ahead, make your wish!"

"Thank you, Grover!" said Big Bird. "My wish for the new year is that everybody all over the world can be friends!"

Then Hoots the Owl played a tune on his sax as everyone celebrated the new year.